BOOK CLUB EDITION

Dr. Seuss's

ABC

Beginner Books

ABCD 3456

BIG A

little   a

What begins with A?

Aunt Annie's alligator

. . . . A . . a . . A

BIG B

little   b

What begins with B?

Barber
baby
bubbles
and a
bumblebee.

BIG

little **C**

c

What begins with C?

Camel on the ceiling
C . . . . c C

BIG D

little   d

David Donald Doo
dreamed
a dozen doughnuts
and
a duck-dog, too.

ABCDE..e..e

ear

egg

elephant

e

e

E

BIG F

little   f

F .. f .. F

Four fluffy feathers
on a
Fiffer-feffer-feff.

ABCD
EFG

Goat
girl
googoo goggles
G . . . g . . . G

BIG H

little   h

Hungry horse.
Hay.

Hen in a hat.
Hooray !
Hooray !

BIG I

little i

i.... i.... i

Icabod
is
itchy.

So am I.

BIG J
little   j

What begins with j?

Jerry Jordan's
jelly jar
and jam
begin that way.

25

BIG K

little k

Kitten. Kangaroo.

Kick a kettle.
Kite
and a
king's kerchoo.

BIG L
little   l

Little Lola Lopp.
Left leg.
Lazy lion
licks a lollipop.

29

BIG M

little   m

Many mumbling mice
are making
midnight music
in the moonlight . . .

mighty nice

BIG N

little n

What begins with those?

Nine new neckties
and a nightshirt
and a nose.

O is very useful.
You use it when you say:
"Oscar's only ostrich
oiled
an orange owl today."

ABCD
EFG
HIJK
LMNO

P

Painting pink pajamas.
Policeman in a pail.

Peter Pepper's puppy.
And now
Papa's in the pail.

BIG Q

little q

What begins with Q ?

The quick
Queen of Quincy
and her
quacking quacker-oo.

QUACK
QUACK

41

BIG R

little   r

Rosy Robin Ross.

Rosy's going riding
on her
red rhinoceros.

BIG S

little s

Silly Sammy Slick
sipped six sodas
and got
sick sick sick.

T....T
t........t

What begins with T?

Ten tired turtles
on a tuttle-tuttle tree.

47

BIG U

little u

What begins with U?

Uncle Ubb's umbrella
and his
underwear, too.

BIG V

little   v

Vera Violet Vinn
 is
very
very
very awful
on her violin.

W . . w . . W

Willy Waterloo
washes Warren Wiggins
who is
washing Waldo Woo.

X is very useful
if your name is
Nixie Knox.
It also
comes in handy
spelling ax
and extra fox.

NIXIE KNOX

BIG Y

little y

A yawning yellow yak.
Young Yolanda Yorgenson
is yelling on his back.

QRS
TUV...

W..X
Y... and ....

BIG Z

little   z

What begins with Z?

I do.

I am a
Zizzer-Zazzer-Zuzz
as you can
plainly see.